THE BOOKMAN

HISTORICAL FICTION BY
HOWARD FAST

**New York   Toronto   London   Auckland   Sydney
Mexico City   New Delhi   Hong Kong**

COVER ILLUSTRATION
GARY CICCARELLI

INTERIOR ILLUSTRATIONS
FRANCIS BAK

Text copyright © 1945 by Howard Fast
Illustrations copyright © 1999 by Scholastic Inc.
All rights reserved. Published by Scholastic Inc. 555 Broadway, New York, NY 10012
by arrangement with Sterling Lord Literistic, Inc.
Printed in the U.S.A.

ISBN 0-439-05688-8

1   2   3   4   5   6   7   8   9   10   23   06   05   04   03   02   01   00   99

TABLE OF CONTENTS

The year is 1780. The American Revolution is on, with the Continentals fighting the British.

CHAPTER 1

We were very poor, but we were never as bad off as the soldiers. Before the war, it had been different. As the war went on, we got poorer and poorer. Yet we were never as poor as the soldiers.

I think it was in the fall of 1780 that the soldiers were all camped down in the valley beyond our house. It was just at the beginning of the winter. The day they came, a film of snow covered the whole valley down to the river.

Our house stood on a hill, overlooking the valley and the river and the plain beyond it. Mother always watched the valley. She said that when father came back, we would see him riding up the valley all the way from the river. Father was with the Third Continentals. He was a captain.

The soldiers came marching down the riverside. They came along the dirt road. Then they turned up the valley, where they prepared to encamp. They were part of the New Jersey line. All of them looked very tired and were very thin. Ann and I ran down to meet them, and they all waved to us. I was ashamed of myself. I was so fat and healthy.

An officer on a horse was riding in front. An aide was riding a little way behind him. When the officer saw us, he came over. He was riding his horse close beside me and leaning over the front of his saddle.

"Hello there, sonny," he said.

I didn't say anything. I thought that maybe he would be thinking how fat I was, he being so thin. His uniform was all torn and dirty. His hat flapped wearily. But I liked his face. It was hard and thin, but it had small, dancing blue eyes.

However, I didn't want him to think me entirely a dunce. I saluted him smartly.

"Well, well," he smiled, "you've the makings of a soldier, haven't you? How old are you?"

"I'm 11, sir."

"And what is your name?"

"Bently Corbatt, sir."

"And I suppose you live in the big house on the hill? Is this your sister?"

"Yes, sir," I replied. "But I've got another, sir."

"Another house?" he questioned, still smiling.

"No, sir. Another sister, who's much bigger than Ann here. And won't you come to the house, sir?"

"You're not Tories, Bently? You don't support the British?"

"Oh no, sir," I said quickly, and then added, "my father's fighting them. He's with the Third Continentals. He's a captain."

"Well," he said, no longer smiling. He stared at me thoughtfully. Then he shifted his gaze to our house. "I'm General Wayne. I suppose you'll be very kind and introduce me to your mother?"

"She's dead, sir."

"I'm sorry. Then your sister, if she's the head of the house."

I nodded. Bending over, he grasped me about the waist, lifting me to the saddle in front of him. Then he motioned for the aide to do the same with Ann. Then we all set off for the house.

"When did your mother die?" he asked me, as we rode along.

"Only about three weeks ago." I told him about how she used to watch the valley all the time. "You see, Father doesn't know yet," I said. "Jane thought it would be best not to let him know."

"I see," he said seriously. But his blue eyes were warm and merry. I don't think his eyes ever lost that merry look.

I twisted around him. That way I could see the troops marching into the valley. Now they were passing through our orchard, and many stooped to pick up rotten apples from the ground. His eyes followed mine. "This business of war is pretty hard for soldiers, isn't it?" He seemed to be including me.

"Not too hard for soldiers," I answered.

Jane was waiting for us on the porch, looking very grave. It was the way she looked since mother had died. We rode up, and the general lifted me down to the porch. Then he got off his horse. He bowed very nicely to Jane, sweeping off his hat with a graceful gesture.

"Miss Corbatt?" the general said.

Jane nodded.

"I am General Wayne of the Continental Army, Pennsylvania line. I have 2,000 troops. I would like to encamp them in that valley. I hope it will be for just a few weeks, but possibly we'll need to stay for a good part of the winter. Is this property yours?"

"Yes." Jane bowed to him. "Yes, the property is ours. Won't you come inside? We can talk about it there."

Do you think that Jane will let the soldiers stay? Why or why not?

The war draws closer and closer . . . and comes in through Bently's front door.

CHAPTER 2

General Wayne entered the house after Jane. His aide followed, and I followed his aide. Ann tried to follow me, but I pushed her back. "This is no place for kids," I told her.

In the living room, I kept very quiet in the corner so I wouldn't be noticed. Jane sat in a chair. The two officers stood in front of her.

"You see," General Wayne was saying, "we can't be too far from the British, and we can't be too near. This spot is ideal."

"I think I understand," Jane replied.

"But you know what soldiers are—2,000 half-starved soldiers," the general warned.

"My father is in the army, sir."

"Thank you. You are a very brave girl."

"No, no," Jane said quickly. "I'm doing nothing. Don't you see that it is safer with the troops here?"

General Wayne smiled sadly. "I'm afraid not. It is not very nice to have one's home turned into a battleground. War is a bitter business."

"I know," Jane said.

"We would like to use your home as general headquarters. It will mean quartering myself and two or three officers."

Jane bent her head. "I hope you will be comfortable," she said.

"You are very kind. And now, if you will excuse me, you can make all the arrangements with Captain Jones here."

The general left the room, and I followed him. Outside, he looked at me curiously.

"I suppose," he said thoughtfully, "that you will want to be a soldier someday?"

"Yes, sir."

His face was very grave, his mouth as thin as a thread. He was clasping and unclasping his hands nervously. "Suppose," he said, "suppose I make you a sort of general's special aide. That way you could look after things I miss."

I was thrilled with pride. I could hardly keep from bursting into shouts of pure joy. However, I managed to stand very still, saluting him. "That will be very fine, sir," I said. And I stood looking after him as he rode down into the valley.

I couldn't go in just yet. I had to stand there for a while, and be alone in my glory. So I remained as he left me, very still, looking over the valley. The sun was setting, giving the river a red glow. Then, after a little time, I went inside.

I heard Jane laughing in the parlor, and it surprised me. It was the first time she had laughed since mother died. I went in, and there she was, standing with the aide. She was laughing at something he had said. When she saw me, she stopped. Captain Jones came forward, offering me his hand.

"How do you do, sir," I said, with dignity.

"How do you do," he answered.

"Captain Jones and General Wayne and some others will live at the house, Bently," Jane told me.

"I know," I replied.

I turned to go, and as I left the room, I heard Captain Jones saying, "I must apologize for my men. We're pretty close to being beggars now—all of us soldiers."

How do you think having soldiers in the house will change life for Bently and Jane? Will they be safer? Or in greater danger?

War is all around him. But it's not what Bently had expected . . . not at all.

CHAPTER 3

The next few days were as exciting as any I had known. I had always thought our house was a very lonely place. There was nobody I could play with outside of Ann and Jack, the caretaker's boy. And now, all of a sudden, there were 2,000 men.

The soldiers were encamped throughout the apple orchard, over the hayfields, and down the long hill to the river. Almost overnight, bubbles of tents had sprung up all over the place.

In and around our sheds 100 horses were quartered. On the lawn, in front of our house, there were 16 cannons, ugly, frightening things. But they were fascinating, too.

I made great friends with many of the soldiers. That was before the bookman came. I will get to the bookman later.

I guess General Wayne spread the word around, about the commission he had given me. The men took to calling me lieutenant, which I was very proud of, though I tried not to show it. I stole cakes and bread for them from the kitchen—not that we had so much, but they had almost nothing at all.

All the time I had to myself, I spent down in the camp. The soldiers were always telling me stories. Sometimes, they would let me handle a musket. But the muskets were taller than I was, and so heavy I could hardly lift them.

What I saw in the camp used to make me sick sometimes. The men were always cold, because they were short of clothing and blankets. Hardly any of them had shoes. Most were terribly thin. It would make me sick. Then I didn't know whether I wanted to be a soldier or not.

The men were always talking about their pay. They said their pay was to come from Philadelphia someday, and how much better everything would be after that.

The winter passed slowly. The men remained in the valley. More men came, until there were almost 3,000 of them. At night, their fires twinkled like glowworms. In the daytime, they were always drilling and parading.

I didn't know why they drilled so much, but one day Captain Jones told me the reason. He said it was to keep them knowing that they were soldiers, and to make them forget that they were starving. I wondered how men could starve, yet live so long. War is very strange, and you do not understand all of it.

Our house became a busy place. In the parlor, General Wayne set up his main headquarters. Sometimes he sat there all day, writing at his desk, receiving messengers and sending messengers, too. I knew that most of his writing was for pay and food for his soldiers, because that was the main topic of talk.

All day, men rode up to our house and away from it. Many times in the night I awoke to hear a horse stamping his hooves in front of the door.

I guess during that time Jane came to sort of like Captain Jones. I guess she couldn't help it. He was such a handsome young gentleman. He was not at all thin and worn, like General Wayne.

Then the bookman came, after the troops had been in the valley for almost three weeks. There aren't many bookmen anymore.

Bookmen are men who wander around the country, stopping at houses to sell books and give away news. Many of them write their own books, publish them, and sell them.

Well, the bookman came early one evening. He came not from the river valley, but instead he rode

the trail that trickled over the hills. He was dressed in worn, rough clothing. He had an old hat on his head, and a very big pack of books on either side of his saddle.

He didn't come to the house. He had stopped at the barn, and I ran over to see what he had to sell. I knew he was a bookman, and I knew how rarely bookmen came these days.

Bently said he didn't know whether or not he wanted to be a soldier. Why? What do you think were the pros and cons?

17

Are books necessary during a war? The bookman says that they are.

CHAPTER 4

"Hello," I called out. "Hello, there, you bookman, you!"

He looked at me very seriously, and right there I liked him. He had little blue eyes, like General Wayne's, always sparkling, and long yellow hair that fell to his shoulders. He couldn't have been much past 30.

"Hello, sir," he said. He had a funny accent. It was vaguely familiar, and I took it to be back-country talk. "Yes," he went on, "how do you do?"

"Fine," I answered. "And I hope you have British books, though Jane says I shouldn't read them now."

"And why shouldn't you read them now?" he asked me.

"You know we're at war."

"Oh, yes, I do know it. I had a tough time getting through the sentries." He spoke as if he didn't approve of the sentries, or war. And then his eyes looked past me, down into the valley. He seemed surprised when he saw all the tents and soldiers. "That looks like a big encampment," he said. "Yes," I said, nodding proudly, "most all of the New Jersey line."

But he did not seem to wish to speak of the troops or the war. "What kind of books do you like?" he asked, measuring me with his eyes.

Then I remembered my manners. "Won't you come in," I asked him, "and have something hot to drink? I am sure my sister would like your books, too."

Picking up his packs, he followed me into the kitchen. I ran to call Jane. Jane liked bookmen, because they made things less lonely.

"I'm sorry," she told him, "that you have to sit in the kitchen, but our house has become a regular military station. I should like to offer you tea, but we have none now."

"You are a very loyal family, aren't you?" the bookman said.

"My father is with the Third Continentals," Jane said quietly.

The bookman looked at her, as though he knew what Jane was thinking. After all, it was much more likely that a strong man like him would be in the army rather than wandering around with a pack of books. And then he said, a slow smile coming to his lips, "But somebody has to sell books. They are as necessary as war."

"Perhaps," Jane answered him.

I went out then, because Ann was calling me. Together we walked down into the valley. When I came back, the bookman was showing Jane all his books.

He and Jane were close together. They were kneeling on the floor, where the books were spread out. There, in the fading twilight, his yellow head made a very nice contrast to Jane's dark one. When I came in, Jane glanced at me.

"Don't you want to look at the books, Bently?"

"I was down in the valley," I said importantly. "I think that the troops are going to move soon, maybe at the end of the week or before that."

The bookman was looking at me very curiously. I thought his interest strange for a person who had so little interest in war. But a moment later, I had forgotten that, and I was looking at the books with Jane. He had a great many books for children. They were exciting books full of pictures, the kind of books we saw very little of at that time.

He seemed to have read every book. He spoke of them in a way different from any other person I had ever known. He spoke of the books Jane wanted, too. I could see that he fascinated Jane, the same way he fascinated me.

I had my dinner, and after dinner, Jane was still with the bookman. They were talking about books and other things. I went out onto the porch where Captain Jones was sitting.

"Who is that tattered wreck?" Captain Jones asked me.

"Oh, he's just a bookman."

"Just a bookman, eh?"

"Yes." I nodded, and then I sat down to keep him company.

Why do you think the bookman is so interested in Bently's talk about the war?

Is war filled with heroes? Bently sees only ordinary men in tattered clothes.

CHAPTER 5

That evening, I sat in the kitchen, listening to the bookman. His stories weren't like the soldiers'. His stories were not about war, but about strange, distant lands. I could see right away that he liked me. I was drawn to him more than I had ever been drawn to a stranger before.

Later, Jane sat before the fire with us. Then most of the talk was between her and the bookman. I remember some of the things he said.

"Egypt is like an old jewel in the sand," he told us. "There are three great pyramids, and they stand all together. . . ."

There seemed to be no land that he had not visited. Although how this should be so with a bookman, neither of us knew.

"And the war . . . ?" Jane once asked him.

"I sometimes wonder about the war," he answered. "But I don't know whether it is right or wrong. This new land is so big, so wild. Why should anyone fight about it?"

"It is a very beautiful land, this America of ours," Jane said.

"Yes, it is," said the bookman.

"Yet you do not believe enough to fight?" Jane asked him.

"Aren't there enough men out there shedding blood?" he replied.

"I suppose so," Jane said.

"I love books," the bookman said. "I used to dream of a great house, where I could live out my days comfortably and slowly. I would have many books around me—and peace."

"I know." Jane nodded.

"Funny, how you dream, isn't it?"

When I went to bed, Jane was still with the bookman. "Good night, Bently," she said.

The bookman shook hands with me. "Don't love war too much, boy," he said.

That night I dreamed of the things the bookman told me. He had to sleep in the barn, since there was no more room in the house. I hoped I would see him the next morning.

The following day, there was more bustle than ever in the camp. All morning it snowed, but the men were out anyway. They were drilling in the snow, and new troops were trickling in all the time.

At the house, General Wayne was in a fury of excitement. I didn't dare go into the parlor.

One day, a tall, tired-looking man rode up with a couple of aides. I heard sentries whispering that it was General Washington. But he did not seem to be the great man I had heard of. He was only a tall, tired-looking person in a patched uniform.

I went to the kitchen to examine the books the bookman had left, and while I was there he came in. I was glad he had not gone. I hoped Jane would like him a great deal and perhaps convince him to remain awhile. I would have been content to listen forever to his smooth voice.

"I want you to read this," he said. It was Mallory's book about King Arthur. I curled up before the fire with it.

Two more days went by. The bookman remained. I noticed that Jane was spending more and more time with him.

Captain Jones did not enjoy this. Once, I had seen the captain with Jane in his arms. And when Jane spoke of him, there was a funny, faraway look in her eyes. Even now, with the bookman there, Jane became more and more downhearted as the time came for the troops to leave.

"But the bookman may remain," I said to her.

"Yes," she answered.

Bently visits the bookman . . . and discovers a horrible secret.

CHAPTER 6

The troops were to leave in the morning. That day they began to break camp. The cannons were wheeled off our lawn, onto the river road. General Wayne was clearing his things from the parlor. I could see he was more excited than usual.

"The old fox has something up his sleeve," one of his sentries told me.

"It wasn't for nothing he was holding that meeting with General Washington," another said.

There was nothing much for me to do. Everyone else was busy, so I went to look for the bookman. I climbed to the little room he had over the hayloft in the barn. I thought I would surprise him. There was a crack in the door, and I looked through it.

There was the bookman, sitting on the floor. He was writing in a little pad he had on his knee. Then I knocked. He seemed to stiffen suddenly. He folded the paper he was writing on and pushed it into the crack in the floor. Then he covered his writing materials with hay. At last he walked to the door. When he saw it was only I, he seemed quite relieved.

"Yes," he said when he had opened the door, "I should be settling things with your sister. I'm going to leave soon, and I want to find out what books she wants."

"You're going?" I said.

"You don't want me to, do you, laddie? But we must all go on a-wandering. Perhaps I'll come back someday soon. . . ."

Walking over to the house with him, I almost forgot about the paper. Then I remembered and excused myself.

Without thinking of what I was doing, I ran back to the barn. I went into his room. I was all trembling with excitement now. I had decided to find out who our bookman really was. I dug up the paper and began to read:

Your Excellency, I have done my best, yet discovered little. There are all of 3,000 troops here now, with 22 cannons. They will be moving north the morning you receive this, possibly to connect with General Washington. . . .

I read on, but my eyes blurred. First I was crying. I was good and ashamed of myself.

Then I realized that the bookman must not find me there. I stumbled down from the loft. I ran out into the snow, the cold air stinging my face. The paper was still in my hand. The whole world was spinning around me.

"Why did it have to be him?" I said.

I guess I went to the kitchen to look at him again. I had to see whether it really was my own, fine bookman who had done this. I opened the door quietly. There was the bookman kissing Jane.

"Go away from here?" she whispered to him. "I don't know . . . I don't know."

"Then I'll tell you. You do love me, but you have too much pride. I'm a tattered wanderer. I have fascinated you with tales. You certainly would be a fool to throw yourself away on someone like me. But you do love me."

"Yes." Jane nodded, and even then I thought that Jane had a lot of dignity.

"I'm not sorry," Jane continued. "Why should I be sorry? I love you. That's all there is to it."

I could see the bookman's face from the side. I don't think I ever saw a sadder face than his. And beautiful, too, with all his yellow hair falling to his shoulders. I don't know how, knowing what I knew,

I could have stood there, watching all this.

"Listen, Jane," the bookman said. "I kissed you once. I won't kiss you again—unless I come back someday. Will you wait?"

"I love you," Jane said. "I know I'll never love anyone else the way I love you."

What has Bently learned about the bookman? What do you think he will do about it?

Bently decides which side he will support—and which side he will betray.

CHAPTER 7

I couldn't stand any more of that. I went up to my room and cried. Then I remembered that a soldier doesn't cry.

General Wayne was in the parlor when I came in. I could see that he was annoyed, being so busy. But he nodded at me.

"What is your business, sir?" he asked.

"Can I ask you something?"

The general pushed his papers aside. Now his eyes were twinkling, and I knew he would take some time with me. He had always liked me.

"Suppose a soldier runs away?" I said.

"There are times when the best do. They have to." The general smiled.

"But suppose he knows his duty is to advance?"

"Then he's a coward—and a traitor," the general said slowly, staring at me very curiously.

"He's a coward, sir?"

"Yes."

I gave him the crumpled piece of paper. But I didn't cry then. I looked straight at him.

"What's this?" He read through it. Then he read through it again. "My heavens," he whispered, "where did you get this?"

I told him. I told him where he could find the bookman. Then I said, "Will you excuse me now, sir?" I knew that something would happen inside me if I didn't get away very quickly.

Why did Bently reveal the truth about the bookman? Was he right to do it? Why or why not?

*Bently did what he had to. And now he has to live
with the consequences. . . .*

CHAPTER 8

They shot the bookman that evening. Captain
Jones tried to keep Jane in the house. "You
mustn't see it," he pleaded with her. "Jane, why
on God's earth should you want to see it?"

"Why?" She looked at him. Then she asked,
"You love me, don't you, Jack?"

"You know it by now," he said.

"And you know what funny things love does to
you. Well, that is why I must see it."

But he didn't understand. Neither did I.

General Wayne came by while they were talking.
He stopped at the group of us. Then he said, "Let
them see it, Captain, if they want to. I don't think
it will hurt Bently. This spy is a brave man."

They stood the bookman up against the side of
the barn. He smiled when they offered to blindfold
him. He asked not to have his hands tied.

"Could I talk to him?" I asked.

"Very well, but not for long."

The bookman had a tired look on his face. Until I got close to him, he had been watching Jane. Then he glanced down at me.

"Hello, laddie," he said.

My eyes were full of tears, so I couldn't see him very well at this point.

"A good soldier doesn't cry," he said, smiling.

"Yes, I know."

"You want to tell me you saw me hide the paper, don't you laddie?"

"Yes."

"And you're sorry now?"

"I had to do it."

"I understand. Give me your hand, laddie."

I went back to Jane after that. She put her arm around me, holding me so tight that it hurt. I was still watching the bookman.

"Sir," the bookman called out, "you will see that my superiors are informed. My name is Anthony Engel. My rank is Brevet Lieutenant Colonel."

General Wayne nodded. The rifles blazed out. The bookman was dead.

Why did Jane want to see the execution? How do you think it changed her life? Bently's life?

DID YOU LIKE THIS BOOK?

Here are two other READ 180 Paperbacks that you might like to read.

THE BEST OF ENCYCLOPEDIA BROWN
What really happened? Who was where when? Who is telling the truth? Use the clues in these stories to solve the mysteries.
BY DONALD J. SOBOL

IT CAME FROM OHIO! MY LIFE AS A WRITER
The true story of R. L. Stine, author of the frighteningly good Goosebumps book collection.
BY R.L. STINE, AS TOLD TO JOE ARTHUR

GLOSSARY

advance	move forward
aide	a person who works along with others to help them do their job
ashamed	embarrassed
blurred	unclear, hard to see
caretaker	someone whose job it is to look after a property
clasping	holding firmly and tightly
commission	a written order giving rank in the armed services
drilling	practicing something over and over again
dunce	someone who doesn't know anything
encamped	settled in a certain place for a while
gesture	an action that shows a feeling
graceful	elegant

grave	serious
hayloft	a platform high above the floor of a barn, where hay is stored
musket	a gun with a long barrel that was used before the rifle was invented
pyramid	a three-sided monument
quartering	providing people, usually soldiers, with food and a place to stay
saluted	raised a hand to the forehead in a gesture of respect
sentries	guards
shedding	letting something fall or drop off
tattered	old and torn
traitor	someone who betrays his or her country
trembling	shaking
twilight	the time of day when the sun starts to set